When Sophie Gets Angry—
Really, Really Angry...

When Sophie Gets Angry— Really, Really Angry...

BY MOLLY BANG

SCHOLASTIC INC.

New York   Toronto   London   Auckland   Sydney
Mexico City   New Delhi   Hong Kong   Buenos Aires

Sophie
was busy
playing
when...

...her sister grabbed Gorilla.

"No!" said Sophie.
"Yes!" said her mother.
"It is her turn now,
Sophie."

Oh,
is Sophie
ever angry
now!

She kicks. She screams. She wants to smash the world to smithereens.

She
roars
a red,
red roar.

Sophie is a volcano,
ready to explode.

And when Sophie
gets angry—
really, really angry...

She runs and runs
and runs until she
can't run anymore.

Then,
for a little while,
she cries.

tweet

Now she sees the rocks,
the trees and ferns.
She hears a bird.

She comes to the
old beech tree.
She climbs.

She feels the breeze
blow her hair.
She watches the water
and the waves.

The wide world
comforts her.

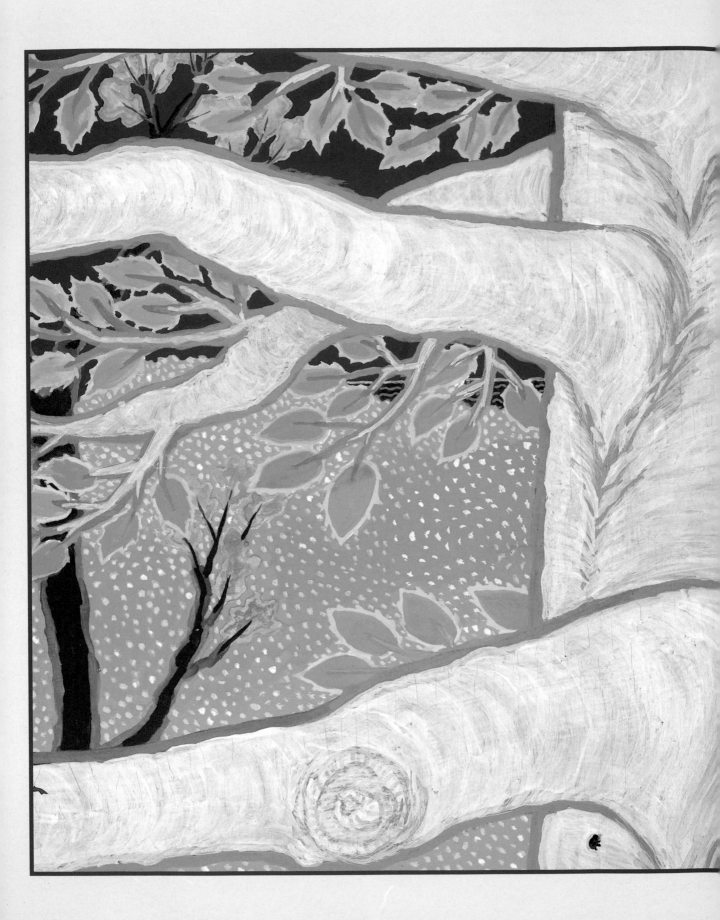

Sophie feels
better now. She
climbs back
down...

...and heads for home.

The house is warm and smells good. Everyone is glad she's home.

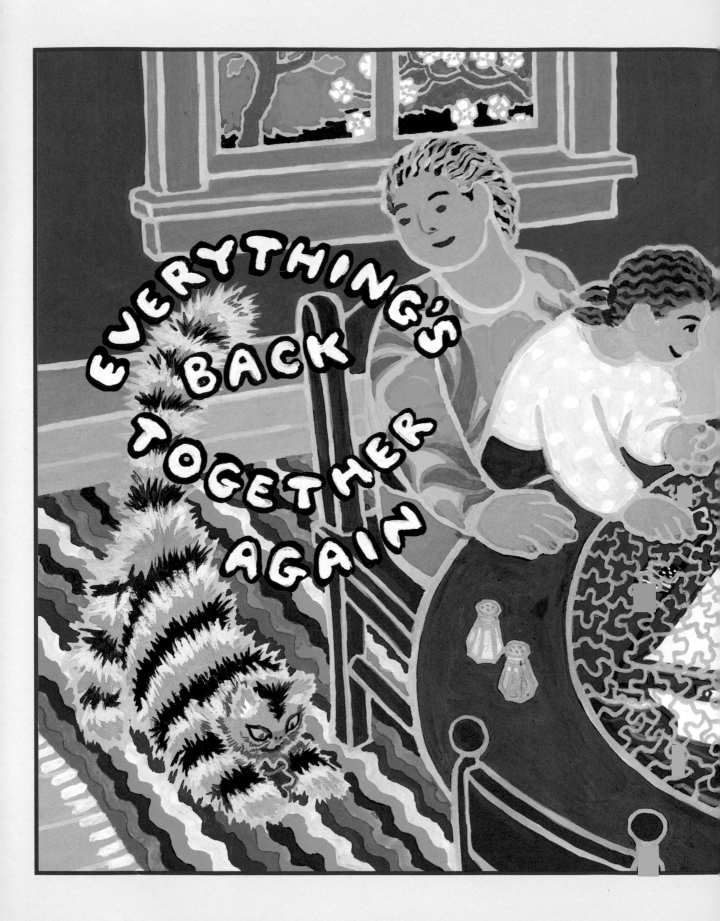

And Sophie
isn't angry
anymore.

To all children, and to all moms and dads,
grandmothers and grandfathers, aunts and uncles and friends,
who ever get angry — even once.
M. B.

When Sophie gets angry, she runs out and
climbs her favorite tree.
Different people handle anger in different ways.

What do you do when you get angry?

ISBN-13: 978-0-439-59845-3
ISBN-10: 0-439-59845-1

Copyright © 1999 by Molly Bang

All rights reserved. Published by Scholastic Inc.
SCHOLASTIC and associated logos are trademarks and/or
registered trademarks of Scholastic Inc.

20 19 18   13 14 15/0
Printed in the U.S.A.   40
First Bookshelf edition, June 2004